Stella Batts

Pardon Me

Praise for Stella Batts:

"Sheinmel has a great ear for the dialogue and concerns of eight-year-old girls. Bell's artwork is breezy and light, reflecting the overall tone of the book. This would be a good choice for fans of Barbara Park's 'Junie B. Jones' books."

— *School Library Journal*

"First in a series featuring eight-year-old Stella, Sheinmel's unassuming story, cheerily illustrated by Bell, is a reliable read for those first encountering chapter books. With a light touch, Sheinmel persuasively conveys elementary school dynamics; readers may recognize some of their own inflated reactions to small mortifications in likeable Stella, while descriptions of unique candy confections are mouth-watering."

— *Publisher's Weekly*

Other books in this series:

Stella Batts Needs a New Name
Stella Batts: Hair Today, Gone Tomorrow
Stella Batts: A Case of the Meanies

Meet Stella and friends online at www.stellabatts.com

Stella Batts

Pardon Me

Book

3

Courtney Sheinmel
Illustrated by Jennifer A. Bell

For Daniel Whelan Moyers
—Courtney

For my good friend Alisa
—Jennifer

Sleeping Bear Press™

315 East Eisenhower Parkway, Suite 200 • Ann Arbor, MI 48108 • www.sleepingbearpress.com
© Sleeping Bear Press, a part of Cengage Learning.

Bubble Wrap® is a registered trademark of Sealed Air Corporation. Life Savers® is a registered trademark of the Wrigley Company, a subsidiary of Mars, Inc. Maltesers® is a registered trademark of Mars, Incorporated. Oreo® is a registered trademark of Kraft Foods. Pop Rocks® is a registered trademark of Zeta Espacial S.A. Red Hots® is a registered trademark of the Ferrara Pan Candy Company. Twizzlers is the product of Y&S Candies, Inc., of Lancaster, Pennsylvania, now a subsidiary of The Hershey Company.

Printed and bound in the United States.
10 9 8 7 6 5 4 3 2 1

Library of Congress Cataloging-in-Publication Data • Sheinmel, Courtney. • Stella Batts : pardon me / written by Courtney Sheinmel ; illustrated by Jennifer A. Bell. • p. cm. • Summary: "Third-grader Stella Batts needs to find a new best friend after her friend, Willa, moves away, but finding a new best friend is not easy" • ISBN 978-1-58536-193-9 (hard cover) — ISBN 978-1-58536-194-6 • (pbk.) • [1. Best friends–Fiction. 2. Friendship–Fiction. 3. Family life–Fiction.] I. Bell, Jennifer A., ill. II. Title. III. Title: Pardon me. • PZ7.S54124Sti 2012 • [Fic]--dc23 • 2012008122

Table of Contents

Carpool

Remember me? I'm Stella Batts. This is my third book. Maybe you've read my first two books. If you haven't, you can start right here.

My mom says if you write at least three books that are all connected then you have a series. So when this book is finished I'll be the author of a series! Hooray!

But so far I'm only on Chapter 1. Here's a list of things that happened since the end of my last book:

1. My best friend, Willa, moved away to Pennsylvania.

2. I changed my favorite color from yellow to blue.

3. My hair grew an eensy weensy bit so it isn't as short as a pixie cut anymore, but it's still not long enough for a ponytail. Sometimes I clip the sides up with barrettes.

Friday afternoons, it's Mom's turn to drive us home from school. "Us" means me, my little sister, Penny, and her best friend, Zoey. It used to mean Willa too, before she moved.

Today Dad's car pulled up in the school parking lot. Mom is pregnant, and her stomach has gotten super big. It's hard for her to squeeze into the driver's seat behind the steering wheel. So Dad has been doing carpool instead. That's another thing that changed since my last book.

After we were all buckled in, Dad started to drive away. "Okay, what game are we playing?" he asked. When Dad carpools, we play car games.

"Geography," I said.

This is how you play Geography. You think of the name of a place, like Arkansas. And then the next person has to use the last letter of your place, which would be an "s." So they could say something like Salt Lake City. The person after that would have to use the "y." It goes on and on until you can't think of any more places.

"I hate that game," Penny said. "Stella

knows more places because she's eight, so it's not fair. How about I Spy?"

You probably already know the game I Spy, but just in case, it's when you say, "I spy with my little eye," and then you describe something you see out the window. Like, "something green," or "something metal." The other players try to guess before we drive by and can't see it anymore.

"We ALWAYS play that game," I said.

"Zoey will be our deciding vote," Dad said.

Penny clasped her hands together and leaned toward Zoey. "Please, pretty please, pick I Spy," she said. "I'll be your best friend."

Zoey giggled. "You already are my best friend," she said. "Okay, it's I Spy."

If Willa were the deciding vote, it would have been Geography, but of course Zoey

picked I Spy.

"Yay!" Penny said. "I'll go first. I spy with my little eye."

"What?" Zoey asked.

"Hold on, I'm still spying."

We drove past Lee Avenue, which is the street Willa used to live on. I knew she wouldn't be there, but I turned my head to look anyway.

"Dad, what time is it?" I asked.

"It's two-fifty," he said.

I had been trying to call Willa, but it's hard because of the time change. Pennsylvania is three hours later than California, which meant it was 5:50 there. That's a good time to call. "Can I use your cell phone please?"

"I'll get it for you at the next red light."

There was a traffic light up ahead, and it turned red just as we got to it. Dad handed me his phone.

"I spy with my little eye something yellow and red," Penny said.

Zoey started guessing as I dialed. I pressed the phone against my ear. Mrs. Getter answered after two rings.

"Hi, it's Stella Batts. Is Willa there?"

"Stella Batts, how lovely to hear your voice. She's just in the other room. Hold on a moment." I heard her put the phone down, and then I heard her call out, "Willa! Stella's on the phone!"

And then I heard Willa say, "I don't want to talk to her."

Those are exactly the words I heard: I don't want to talk to her.

But I knew I must have heard her wrong. Why wouldn't Willa want to talk to me? I didn't do anything wrong.

Or did I? I thought about the things we

did before Willa left Somers. We played a hundred games of Spit, we had a bunch of sleepovers, we went to Brody's Grill and sat by ourselves at the table. We never fought. She was never mad at me, not once!

Mrs. Getter picked up the phone again. "I'm sorry, Stel. We're headed out for a picnic dinner, but I'll make sure she calls you back another time."

A picnic with Willa in the redwood forest had been number 4 on my wish list of things to do before Willa moved away, but we didn't have time to go. Now she was going without me—not to the redwood forest, but somewhere in Pennsylvania. Maybe somewhere she liked even better. And she wouldn't even talk to me first. That seemed kind of mean. I didn't understand. Willa is NEVER a meanie.

Is it possible that she moved to

Pennsylvania and turned mean? Oh no, I hoped not.

Mrs. Getter said goodbye. I heard the phone click when she hung up. I kept the phone pressed to my ear for a few more seconds, just waiting. Maybe Willa would come to the phone after all. But I knew the line was dead and she really wouldn't.

"Willa wasn't there?" Dad asked when I finally handed the phone back to him.

"She's going on a picnic," I said.

"Hurry up and guess!" Penny said. "You didn't guess yet, and it's about to be too late!"

"I don't want to play," I said.

"Then I win," Penny said. "It was the lady in the car next to us. She had a yellow and red clip in her hair, and her car just turned down that street."

"That was a good one, Pen," Dad said.

Now we were on Zoey's street, and Dad pulled up in front of her house. Zoey's mom came out to meet her. Dad rolled down the window to talk to her for a couple of minutes, because Zoey and Penny are having a play date on Saturday and they needed to decide what time.

I clicked my heels three times, which is what I do when I want to make a wish, but I didn't know exactly what to wish for.

After that we drove away. We were going to Batts Confections so that Penny and I could see the candy garden one last time. Dad said it was time for a change, so he's taking out the garden and putting in a candy circus. I would have put it on my list of things that have changed since my last book, except it hasn't changed quite yet.

Batts Confections is in an outdoor

shopping center. There wasn't a parking spot in front of our store, so we parked near Man's Best Friend. That's a pet store 109 steps away. Once I counted. "Give a Home to a Pet Who Needs One," read the sign by the door. Penny ran right up to see the window dogs—you know, the dogs they keep in the cage in the window.

Dad and I walked up behind Penny. There was only one window dog and she was curled

up so the top of her head was nestled right by her toes. All you saw was her white fur, like she was a marshmallow. She was kind of a big marshmallow, but still an eensy weensy dog.

The sign in front said "Maltese." When I was Penny's age, which is five, I thought those signs were nametags. Now I know it just means the kind of dog. Like I'm a human, but my name isn't "Human."

I couldn't remember ever seeing a Maltese before. It made me think of the malted things we sell at Batts Confections. Malt balls, Maltesers, malted milkshakes.

"Can we go in and look at the other dogs?" Penny asked.

Before Dad had a chance to answer, the door opened and two people came out—a woman and a girl. The girl was tall enough to be at least ten years old. She was dressed like a grown-up. Instead of jeans, she had on slacks, and a white blouse tucked in. She was holding the woman's hand, but she dropped it as soon as they stepped out onto the sidewalk, and she ran up to the window.

"C'mon, let's go," the woman called.

"Not until you promise we're coming back."

"Fine, I promise."

"When, Mom?"

She was speaking with an accent, and actually she didn't say "Mom." She said "Mum." I happen to know that's the way they say "Mom" in some other countries.

"After lunch," her mom said. "In about forty-five minutes or so."

Her mom DIDN'T have an accent. How weird is that? Aren't kids supposed to sound like their parents? Maybe she was just pretending to have an accent. Willa and I did that sometimes, but ours never sounded as real as this girl's did.

"And then we'll play with her?"

"Yes."

"Forty-five minutes, and then we'll play with you, sleepyhead," the girl said, still with an accent. They started to walk toward Brody's Grill, which is the restaurant in the shopping center, and I heard the girl say, "Can I have a plate of chips for lunch?" A plate of chips? Didn't she mean a bag of chips?

Penny tugged on my arm. "C'mon, let's go," she said.

CHAPTER 2

We'll See

When you walk into Man's Best Friend, there are more cages. Each cage has a sign on the side so you know what kind of puppy is inside.

"Hey, what kind are those?" Penny asked. She pointed to a cage at the end of the second row with one brown puppy and one black one.

"It says Chow Chow," I told her.

"One Chow and another Chow?" Penny asked.

"Nope, they're each a Chow Chow," Dad

told her. "It's a name so great you have to say it twice."

"Why are they different colors?" Penny asked.

"Because Chow Chows come in different colors," Dad said.

"It's a weird name for a dog," I said, "since you can chow down on food."

"That's true," Dad said. "I can't wait to chow down on the brussels sprouts Mom is making for dinner tonight."

"Oh gross, really?" I said, at the same time Penny said, "Yummy!" She actually LIKES brussels sprouts.

"Really," Dad told me. "But if you promise you'll eat at least five of them, you can pick out something at Batts Confections to bring home for dessert. Are you girls ready?"

"No," I said. "I want to see if we can play

with a dog."

"We can play with a dog?" Penny asked.

"I think so," I said. "That other girl said she was going to."

"What other girl?" Dad asked.

"The girl with the accent," I said.

"Maybe she was going to adopt one," Dad said. "We're not going to be getting a dog today."

What he meant was, we're not going to be getting a dog ANY day. My mom doesn't like them. I mean, she really REALLY doesn't like them. I keep telling her that dogs are man's best friend—man short for human, which includes women too. But Mom says Aunt Laura is her best friend, and not some dog that would shed all over the furniture and chew up our shoes.

"Please Dad, can we just ask? I already

know which one I want to play with," I said.

"Not the Chow Chow," Penny said. "If it gets really hungry and there's no food, it might decide to chow down on my fingers."

"No," I said. "I want the one in the window."

Dad turned to look at the little Maltese again. "That's a cute dog, Stel," he said.

"That's the one I want too," Penny said, copying me like she always does, but this time it was okay.

Dad waved at the pet store man so he knew to come over to us.

"Are you thinking about adopting a puppy today?" the man asked.

"Yeah, the Maltese," Penny said. "We might buy it."

"Now, now, Pen," Dad said. "You know we're not going to do that."

"You said we're not getting a dog *today*, but you didn't say not ever," Penny told him. "You could get me one on a special day, like on my birthday."

"We'll see," Dad said.

I'm old enough to know that *We'll see* really just means no. But Penny still thinks that it might mean yes.

"The Maltese is popular today," the pet store man said. "But it looks like she's still taking a nap and we don't like to disturb the puppies when they're sleeping. She's pretty tired after the ride from the shelter this morning. Is there another dog you're interested in?"

"Stel?" Dad asked.

But suddenly Penny called out. "Look! It opened its eyes!"

I looked and sure enough, the Maltese

had uncurled from her little white ball and her eyes were open. "Looks like she wants to play with you after all," the pet store man said. "Give me a minute, and I'll meet you back in the playroom with her. It's all the way down the aisle and to your left."

How cool is it that there's a playroom for you to play with the puppies?!

In case you're wondering, this is what

was inside the pet playroom: two red plastic chairs for people to sit on, a blue rubber ball, and a roll of paper towels. The pet store man came in with the Maltese and set her down on the floor. "I'll be back in a few minutes," he said. "You can shout for me if you need me to take her back sooner."

"Thank you," Dad said.

Penny threw the blue ball and called, "Fetch!" But the puppy didn't move.

"I don't think she knows any tricks yet," Dad said.

"Then I'll just hold her," Penny said. She reached down to grab the puppy, and it scooted across the room and into the corner.

"She doesn't like me," Penny said.

"You're just a giant to her," Dad said.

"I'm not a giant," Penny said. "I'm the shortest person in here." That was true. Penny is just barely shorter than I am, but it still counts.

"If I did this I'd be a giant," Penny said, and she climbed up on one of the red chairs and waved her hands around. "I'm a giant now."

"Be careful, Pen," Dad said. "Here, watch this." He made a fist, and bent down toward the dog. She took a couple of steps toward him and sniffed. I saw her pink tongue, like an eensy weensy stick of gum, dart out of her mouth and lick Dad's knuckles.

"Ew," Penny said, as she hopped down from the chair. "She licked you."

"It's just the puppy way of shaking hands," Dad said.

"Can I try?" I asked.

"Of course," Dad said.

I made a fist, just like he did, and the

puppy sniffed it. She licked me too, but her tongue was so tiny I could barely feel it. Then slowly, slowly, I moved my hand to the top of her head and petted her. She turned her head a little bit, so I could tell she wanted me to pet her some more. Her fur was soft, like a stuffed animal. When I picked her up, she was lighter even than Belinda, Penny's stuffed platypus. It was like holding cotton candy, except not sticky at all. "Hi there, little puppy-pup," I said in a baby voice.

"She looks content," Dad said.

"What does that mean?" Penny asked.

"It means she's happy that I'm holding her," I said.

"She'll be happy with me too," Penny said. "It's my turn." She put her arms out.

Dad nodded at me, so I knew I had to hand her over. I kissed the fluffy top of the puppy's head and gave her to Penny. "Be careful," I said when Penny squeezed her. "You might hurt her."

"I'm just hugging her like you did," Penny said. See how she copies me? And I was right about Penny hurting her, because the puppy started whimpering.

"Put her down and let her sniff you," Dad said.

Penny did, even though you could tell she really didn't want to. I scooped the puppy back up in my arms.

"Stella's not being fair," Penny whined. "It's my turn for her to sniff me."

"She can sniff you while I hold her," I said.

Penny held out her fist. At first the puppy didn't even seem to notice. But after a few seconds she started sniffing, and her tongue came out again. Then Dad said, "Girls, it's just about time to go."

"First can I try holding her again?" Penny asked. "Please?"

I looked at Dad and he nodded, so I handed the puppy over. "Don't hurt her," I said.

"I know, I know," Penny told me.

I watched her cradle the little pup in her arms. She rocked her back and forth, the way she does with Belinda sometimes. But Belinda is a stuffed animal, so it doesn't bother her when Penny squeezes her and rocks her like that. I'm not sure my puppy liked it.

Okay, I know she wasn't really MY puppy, but she liked me best so it kind of seemed that way.

After a couple of minutes Dad said it was REALLY time to go. The pet store man walked back in to take the puppy away. She had to go back to her cage, poor little pup. She didn't even have a cage friend. And I could tell she wanted to be my new best friend, because she was meant to be mine.

CHAPTER 3

Raining Cats & Dogs

Penny and I picked out flower lollypops at
Batts Confections. We wanted the ones from
the candy garden, but Dad said those pops
were probably dirty from being on display
for so long, so we took the mini chocolate
lollypops they sell on the Penny Candy Wall.
We also got cookie dough, which is a new
thing they're selling at the store. Then we
went home.

"Stella!" Penny called.

I didn't answer her because I was helping Mom choose which brussels sprouts to put on my plate. The big ones are SUPER gross. The littler ones are gross too, but only medium gross. If I had to eat five of them, I wanted to make sure Mom only gave me the little ones.

"Hurry up, Stella!" Penny called.

"Those two are very small," Mom said, pointing to the littlest ones I'd picked out—the least gross of all, if you asked me. "How about if I give you one more."

I shook my head. "That would be six and Dad promised just five," I said.

"Stell-ahhhhh!!!" Penny called again. This time she made the last syllable drag out for a really long time, which is how she says my name when she really REALLY wants me to do something.

"Go see what she wants," Mom said. "I'll finish up."

"Just five," I reminded Mom.

"All right," she said.

"I'm coming," I called back to Penny, and I went from the kitchen through the dining room to the den.

Penny had dragged in four of the dining room chairs, and put one at each corner of a blanket spread out in the middle of the floor.

"What are you doing?" I asked.

"You said Willa was going on a picnic for dinner, so I thought we should too. But Dad said we couldn't because it would be too hard for Mom to sit on the ground and then stand back up again."

Sitting down and standing up are two more things that are hard for Mom since she's pregnant.

"Dad said I could set up a picnic for just us in here," Penny continued.

"Why did you bring four chairs if it's only two of us?"

"It's THREE of us," Penny said. "You forgot Belinda."

"Okay THREE of us," I said. "But there are still FOUR chairs."

"Stella, it's a picnic," she said slowly, like I was the younger sister and she was the older one, and she had to explain things to me. "You don't sit on chairs at a picnic. They're posts for the tent."

"You don't have tents at a picnic either," I said.

"Yeah, but it looks like rain and we don't want the food to get all wet. Just look at the sky." She held her arm up toward the ceiling. "Rain clouds."

The ceiling in the den is painted white. It looked the way it always did, not sunny or cloudy because it's inside the house. But I decided to play along. Sometimes that's what big sisters have to do. "You're right," I said. "The clouds are super dark too."

"It's going to be a big storm," Penny said.

"I know." I pointed to the lamp in the

corner. "Look how the trees are shaking in the wind.

Penny crossed her arms like she was trying to keep warm. "Brrrr," she said.

"We need shelter. I'll help you pitch the tent," I told Penny.

I got a sheet from the hall closet—the big kind that fits on Mom and Dad's bed. We stretched it out across the tops of the chairs and climbed underneath. Of course Belinda came too.

"Don't be scared," Penny told her. "It's safe and cozy in here."

Dad brought us our food. We could tell which plate was meant for Penny because she had more sprouts. "If we're stranded here, this could be the last food we ever eat," I told her.

She speared one of her sprouts with her fork. "Oh, brussels sprout, I love you so much.

I wish I had more of you."

Maybe brussels sprouts taste different in Penny's mouth than in mine. How else could she like them so much?

We finished eating and pushed our plates out of the way. "It's still thundering out there," Penny said. "Belinda's afraid of thunder. And she's cold and hungry." She pulled her onto her lap and cradled her just like she'd cradled the puppy.

"I wonder what Malty is doing right now,"

I said.

"Malty?"

"The Maltese from Man's Best Friend," I said. "Her name is Malty for short. I made it up just now."

"Oh no!" Penny cried. "She's out in the rain! We have to go look for her!"

"I'll go," I said. I crawled out of the tent and looked around the den, like she actually might've been hiding under the coffee table or behind the couch, even though I knew she wasn't.

I headed to the dining room. "Have you guys seen Malty?"

"Who?" Mom asked.

"The puppy from Man's Best Friend," I told her. "She's the cutest puppy EVER! Even you would like her!"

"A cute puppy that even I would like–I'll

keep an eye out for her. Did you girls finish dinner?"

"Yup," I said.

"Including all five sprouts?"

I nodded.

"Okay, you can have dessert," Mom said. "The lollypops are on the counter by the sink."

"What about the cookie dough?"

"When Dad and I finish up dinner, we can make the cookies."

I went into the kitchen and grabbed a couple of lollypop flowers–one for me and one for Penny–off the counter. Then I headed back to the den and ducked back under the sheet. "I found her!" I said. "Malty was sitting outside the tent the whole time!" I announced.

"Oh thank goodness," Penny said. "I was so worried." She moved her hand through the air like she was petting a puppy.

"And I picked some flowers for us to eat in case we get hungry again," I said. I handed her one of the lollypops. "Some flowers are poisonous, but these are safe."

"How can you tell for sure?"

"See this special pattern on the petals," I said, pointing to the pink swirls that are really peppermint. Penny nodded. "That means they won't make you sick," I told her.

We ate our lollypops. Penny offered a lick to Belinda, so I held mine out to the air and let Malty have a taste. "Not too much, little malt ball," I said. "You don't want to get a stomachache."

Penny reached up and pulled at the sheet. "The wind and the rain are making the tent cave in!" she said.

"Oh no!" I said, reaching up and pulling at it too. It slipped off the backs of the chairs and came down on our heads. We both stood up and jumped around underneath it.

"Help us! Our tent caved in!" we shouted.

"Girls!" Mom said.

After that she made us clean everything up, including folding the sheet and the blanket back up, which was not easy to do. And we didn't get to make the cookies, because when we finished cleaning, it was almost time for bed.

Here's something I've learned: Cleaning up ALWAYS takes more time than making the mess does.

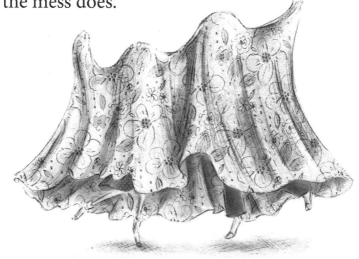

CHAPTER 4

The Surprise

The next morning, Maverick came over. He's the boy who lives in the house behind us. There's a hole in the fence in between our houses. When he comes over, he knocks on the sliding glass door to the kitchen instead of the front door.

Maverick told us his parents were making pancakes for breakfast, and he invited Penny and me to come. But when we got there, they tasted funny. Mrs. Finch (that's Maverick's mom) said she used whole-wheat flour, instead of regular flour, because it's healthier.

"How about chocolate chips?" I asked. "My dad always adds those in."

"Sorry, Stella," Mrs. Finch said. "No chocolate chips. But we do have raisins, if you want."

I shook my head. Raisins are almost as bad as brussels sprouts! Next time, breakfast will be at our house.

Afterwards, Penny and I went home. "Mom! Daddy!" Penny shouted. "We're back! Where are you?"

"I'm in here," Mom called out.

We followed her voice into the room that right now is still the guest room, but soon it's going to be the baby's room.

It already looked different than it used to

look. Instead of a big bed, there's a crib and a mini couch that Mom says is called a love seat. There's also a new dresser. It's tan, the same color as the crib, and it has a shelf on top where you put the baby when you have to change its diaper. Mom and Dad say we'll get to help out when the baby is born, but diaper changing is NOT going to be my job!

Mom was standing next to the dresser, folding clothes and putting them inside the drawers.

"More baby stuff?" I asked.

"Onesies," she said, holding up a shirt that attached at the bottom, so it was like a shirt and underwear all in one. "Aunt Laura and Uncle Rob sent them over."

The baby has been getting a bunch of presents even though it's not born yet. Actually, the baby isn't an "it." It's a boy. First

his name was going to be Teddy, then it was going to be Cooper. Now Mom and Dad say he'll be Daniel. Still, Aunt Laura and Uncle Rob don't even know him. They know Penny and me, and they didn't send us anything.

It makes me kind of jealous even though the presents aren't anything I'd want. What would I do with rattles or baby clothes?

"Where's Dad?" Penny asked.

"He went to the store," Mom said.

"So what are we going to do?"

"You can help me fold the baby clothes, and then you're having a play date with Zoey."

"Oh, I forgot I'm getting to see Zoey! Oh, hooray!"

Penny did a happy little dance right there in the guest room/baby's room. I wished Willa were coming over too. Just thinking about her made me miss her. I wondered how her picnic was. If only she still lived in Somers, she could've come on our den

picnic and slept over and had breakfast at Maverick's house.

But Willa moved to Pennsylvania and didn't want to talk to me anymore. She wasn't my best friend anymore.

"You look sad, Stel," Mom said. "Don't worry. We'll think of something special for you to do."

"I wish I'd gone to the store with Dad," I said. If I went to the store, I'd get to pass Man's Best Friend, and if I passed Man's Best Friend, I'd get to see Malty. Will you take me?"

"It's hard for me to fit my body into the driver's seat right now," Mom said. "You understand, right?"

"Yeah," I said glumly. "Is it okay if I call Dad?"

Mom said yes and I went into the other room to get the phone. "Can you come and get me?" I asked when he answered.

"Ah, you miss your old dad?"

"Yeah," I said.

Okay, that wasn't exactly true. I didn't miss Dad right then, but I did want to be with him because he was near Malty, and Malty was the closest thing I had to a best friend.

"Well you're in luck," Dad said. "I'll be home soon and I have a surprise for you when I get there."

"What is it?"

"It's a surprise."

"Is it candy?"

"Nope, it's nothing edible," he said.

"I have an idea," I said. "Can you tell me the surprise in the car?"

"You know I can't talk on the phone when I'm driving," Dad said.

"No, I meant can you come here and pick

me up and take me to Man's Best Friend and tell me about the surprise on the way?"

"You want to go to Man's Best Friend again?"

"I want to play with Malty."

"I don't know if they'll let you play with her," Dad said. "Someone bought her, so she'll be going to her new home soon."

"You mean I'm never going to see her again?"

"Well, never say never," Dad said. "And just so you know, I have it on good authority that she's going to end up in a good home."

"What's authority?"

"Someone in a position to know things," Dad said.

"So who is it?"

"You'll see," Dad said.

You'll see is kind of like *We'll see.*

But suddenly I thought about something: What if *You'll see* means more than maybe? What if it means yes? As in, *Yes, you can have a dog?!!!*

I started to understand all the things Dad had said, like, "Never say never." Obviously! I was going to see Malty again because she was going to live with us! "I have it on good authority that she ended up in a good home."

He was the authority, and the good home was our home!

"I'm getting into the car right now," Dad said. "We'll talk about this when I get home."

"I can't wait!" I said.

Except that it took SEVEN MILLION HOURS for Dad to get home. Okay, not really, but that's what it felt like.

Finally I heard the garage door open and I went out to meet him. He didn't even have time to get out of the car before I ran up and started looking in all the windows.

"Where is she?" I asked.

"Who?"

"My surprise."

"How do you know your surprise is a person?"

A person? Didn't he mean a dog? And specifically, didn't he mean Malty the dog?

Wait a second. *Maybe* he said "person" because he wanted to confuse me. That way the surprise would be even bigger. He probably arranged for someone to be watching my puppy right then, like Stuart, who works at our store. Soon Stuart would come over with Malty. She'd have a big red bow around her neck. Oh, this was going to be so great! I couldn't wait!

"Come on," Dad said. "Let's go inside and I'll tell you all about it."

We walked back toward Mom and Penny. I was trying to decide what look to put on my face so Dad would think I really was surprised when he finally told me. Don't your eyes get wide when you're surprised? I widened my eyes, just to practice.

"Your face looks funny," Penny said.

"No it doesn't," I said. I blinked quickly

and opened them the regular way.

"Stel," Dad said, "are you ready to hear about your surprise?"

"Yes!" I said.

"Do I have a surprise too?" Penny asked.

Dad shook his head. "This time the surprise is for Stella," Dad said.

"That's not fair," Penny said. "Then you have to make Stella share with me."

I hoped they didn't make me share too much. After all, Malty didn't even really like Penny.

"You don't even know what it is yet," Dad said. But Penny's mouth was already down in a pout. "Stella, I'm going to take you over to someone's house to play."

"That's my surprise?" I asked. (By the way, I'm sure I really did look surprised, because it wasn't at all what I was expecting. And not in

a good way.)

But Dad was nodding and smiling. "A woman came into the store this morning. I heard her telling Stuart that she just moved to Somers and she has a daughter in the third grade who's in need of a playmate. I told her I had a third grader in need of a playmate too."

"You shouldn't have said that. Now she'll

think I don't have any friends."

"I'm sure she won't think that," Mom said. "After all, her daughter didn't have someone to play with today either."

"But it's different because she just moved here." I said.

"She'll just be happy you're coming over," Dad said. "Her mother is excited to meet you too."

"What about me?" Penny asked.

"You're having a play date with Zoey," Mom reminded her.

"Oh yeah," Penny said.

"What's the girl's name?" I asked.

"Evie," Dad said.

"I've never known anyone with that name before," I said.

"Well there's a first time for everything," Dad said. "So should I drop you off, darling?"

"Do I have to go?" I asked. This girl, Evie, was a stranger. What if Dad dropped me off and I didn't even like her?

"You don't have to go," Dad said. "But why not? You don't have anything else planned today, and Penny has Zoey coming over."

You see, even Dad thought I had no friends.

CHAPTER 5

Good Things Come in Small Packages

Evie lives in a part of Somers called Hilltop Acres. It's just five blocks from our house, so Dad and I walked—just like Penny can walk to Zoey's because she lives so close. On the way over, I changed my mind about the whole thing. I like dogs just fine, but a HUMAN would be my first choice for a best friend. Maybe Evie would be the right human new best friend for me.

Hilltop Acres has a bunch of really

loooooong buildings, and each one has twelve front doors—I counted—twelve different homes. Dad told me they're called garden apartments.

We walked up to apartment 307. I pressed the button to ring the doorbell. "Coming," a lady's voice called from the other side.

I was excited and nervous all at the same time and I reached for Dad's hand. He took it and squeezed my hand back. But holding my dad's hand seemed a little babyish, so I pretended all I wanted was the squeeze and I let go right before the door swung open.

I recognized the lady on the other side right away. She was the one who had been at Man's Best Friend, who had the daughter with an accent. "Hello Dave," she said in a no-accent kind of voice. She turned to me. "And you must be Stella. I'm Julie King. It's nice to meet you."

Dad nudged me in the side just the eensy weensiest bit. "Nice to meet you too," I said.

"Come on in, and please excuse the mess." She held the door open wider. We stepped inside and I saw there were tons of boxes. They all had writing on the sides, like "J. Sweaters," "E. Books," "H. Papers," and "Bathroom."

"Evie!" Mrs. King shouted. The girl with the accent came when Mrs. King called, just like I knew she would.

"This is my daughter, Evie," Mrs. King said. "We just moved here from England, and she's going to be in Mrs. Finkel's third-grade class on Monday."

"Stella's in Mrs. Finkel's class too," Dad said.

It was hard to believe Evie was in my grade. She was even taller than I remembered. Like if you stacked two Batts bars the long way on top of my head, that's how tall she was. She was wearing a red plaid skirt, a white shirt, and a vest that was the same red plaid as the skirt. I felt like I wasn't dressed up enough to play with her.

"Wonderful," Mrs. King said. "I don't think Evie's unpacked all her games yet, but you'll have a lot to talk about."

"Do you have a deck of cards?" I asked. I turned to Evie. "I could teach you to play Spit."

"That's gross," she said.

"It's not really spit," I started to explain.

"No thank you," she said.

"Well, I'm sure you girls will work something out," Dad said. "So, Stel, I'll pick you up in a couple of hours, okay?"

I started to say, "Okay."

"Hold on," Evie said. "We're supposed to play for a couple of HOURS?"

"Evie!" Mrs. King said.

"What?" she said. "I've got a lot of unpacking to do. And I promised Tesa I'd ring her, too."

Ring? Did she mean call?

It didn't matter what she meant. This girl was NOT going to be my new best friend.

"You're being rude," Mrs. King told her. She turned to Dad and me. "Tesa is a friend from London," she explained. "I grew up here in Somers, but Evie is having some trouble adjusting."

"I'm not having trouble adjusting," Evie said. "I just have other stuff to do and I don't want to play with her."

My cheeks went hot, really hot, so I knew they were turning red: red like cherry Life Savers. Red like Twizzlers. Red like red hot candies. First Willa, then Evie. Okay, so Willa didn't exactly say "I don't want to play with her." But "I don't want to talk to her" is close enough.

Evie and her mom glared at each other. I waited for Dad to say it was time for us to go home, but right then someone pushed open the door from the outside and almost banged Dad on the head.

It was a man. A SUPER tall man. Like if three Evies stood on top of one another, that's how tall he was.

"Hey, I'm sorry mate," the man said. His accent was just like Evie's. Well, not just like hers–he had the grown-up man version of her voice. But still, unlike Mrs. King, he sounded like someone who was related to Evie.

"My husband, Hugh," Mrs. King said to me and Dad. We all said, "Nice to meet you."

"Sorry again about the door," Mr. King said. "I'm having a bit of bad luck today. I've just locked the keys to the truck inside the truck. We don't have a spare set, do we Jules?"

"Again?" Mrs. King asked. "Why is it so hard for you to remember your keys?"

"I guess I'm busy remembering to drive on the right side of the road," he said.

Mr. King can't remember what side of the road to drive on? I will NEVER get into a car with him! Not that I'll ever have to, because Evie and I aren't going to be friends.

"My wife was able to open a car door with a wire hanger once," Dad said.

"I didn't know that," I said. "When?"

"Last year, a customer locked her keys in the car. Mom saved the day."

"Evie, can you fetch me a wire hanger?" Mr. King asked. Fetch is something you'd tell a dog to do. I'd never heard anyone ask a human being to fetch anything before. Maybe that's what they say in England to people, and something else to dogs.

Evie went off to find a hanger and came back a couple of minutes later. "How's this?"

"That's perfect," Dad said, taking it from her. We all headed outside to the truck.

"I see your keys, Dad," Evie said.

(I guess there's no special word that means "dad" in England, even though they say "mum" instead of "mom.")

"I know, I see them too," Mr. King said. I stood on my tiptoes to see, but I was still too short. Dad straightened out the wire hanger except for the hook part on top, and he jabbed it down into the bottom of the window. I waited for the door to pop open, but nothing happened. Dad pulled the hanger out and tried again. Again, nothing. It didn't work the third or the fourth time either.

"I'm sorry, Hugh," Dad said.

"That's all right, mate," Hugh said. He put a hand to his forehead and closed his eyes, like he was thinking hard. "If only the window in the back were wider, I'd crawl through it and open the door from the inside."

I glanced over. The window in the back of the truck was the kind that slides open and shut across, not up and down. No way Mr. King could fit through it. Aside from being super tall, he had a kind of big stomach. I'm not saying that to be mean. It's just the truth. And the window was small. Really REALLY small.

"You know," Dad said, "I bet Stella could fit through that window."

I wished he hadn't said that. Now everyone would be thinking about how I was the littlest one.

Mr. King looked down at me. He seemed even taller than before. I felt even shorter.

Dad looked down at me, too. "What do you think, darling? Want to try going through the window?"

My heart started beating harder, like

THUMP THUMP THUMP. The window seemed even smaller than before. Windows can't shrink, can they? What if I got stuck halfway in and halfway out?

I thought about *Superstar Sam,* my favorite show. Sam's gymnastics coach always tells her, "When the going gets tough, the tough get going." Sam would DEFINITELY try going through the window.

"Okay," I told Dad.

"Atta girl," Dad said.

"Splendid," Mr. King said.

Dad lifted me up into the back of the truck and then he climbed in after me. There were a bunch of paint cans, and other painting supplies, like those big roller brushes and a tarp. We had to climb around everything to get to the window. Dad slid the window as open as it would go. He told me to lift my arms

up, like the way you do when you're going to dive into a pool, and put them through. So I did. He held onto my legs and pushed me slowly, slowly, slowly. I guided myself with my hands, gripping the seats as I went. My side got scraped a little bit as I dropped down onto the seat.

The keys were right there on the front seat. I pulled up the little knob to unlock the door and Mr. King opened it up wide. "Well done!" he said. Mrs. King clapped her hands, and Evie did, too.

I hopped down from the front seat. Dad was back on the sidewalk and he squeezed me to him. "Good job, darling," he said.

Mr. King pulled his wallet out of his pocket. "This deserves a reward. How about a dollar?"

"That's not necessary, Hugh," Dad said. "Right Stel?"

I shook my head, even though I think I really deserved the dollar because I had the scrape on my side. It was starting to hurt a little bit.

"Good things come in small packages, now don't they?" He patted the top of my head, like I was a puppy.

"That was really amazing," Evie said, smiling. And just like that, she started to like me.

"How about ice cream for all?" Mr. King asked.

I didn't answer, because what if Evie still wanted to ring her friend Tesa, whatever that meant? But then Evie said, "Yes!"

So we all went. Even Mrs. King, who took a break from unpacking, and even Dad. "You can carpool to school with us if you want," I told Evie. It was Mrs. Benson's turn to drive to school. She's Penny's friend Zoey's mom. I was sure she wouldn't mind.

"I'll be taking Evie on Monday," Mrs. King said. "There are a lot of forms to fill out for the first day."

"So you'll see each other in school then," Dad said.

I grinned across the table at Evie. We sure would.

CHAPTER 6

Pardon Me

Evie was going to be my new best friend! I was sure of it!

On Monday, I was the most excited I'd ever been about going to school.

Mom had Penny and me waiting by the front door at 7:55 a.m., the same as always. But Mrs. Benson didn't get there until 8:02. How could she be late when it was SO IMPORTANT for me to be on time, or even early?

Finally she pulled up and we ran out.

"Sorry girls," Mrs. Benson said. "It's been one of those days. First I spilled coffee on myself, so I had to change my shirt. Then I couldn't find my keys."

People sure were having a lot of problems with keys.

"Buckle up," Mrs. Benson said. "We should still make it in time."

There are a bunch of different ways to get to school from my house. Mom always turns down Parrot Avenue because it's shorter, and Mrs. Benson always drives up Tollridge Street because there aren't any traffic lights. So we drove down our street and made a right at the end of the block. Then we made a left on Tollridge. Suddenly, Mrs. Benson stopped the car.

"Mo-om," Zoey whined.

"It's not my fault, Zo," Mrs. Benson said. "There's a garbage truck ahead of us."

I didn't say anything, even though it WAS kind of Mrs. Benson's fault. She was the one who spilled her coffee and lost her keys. If not, she would have left her house on time and picked us up on time. We would've gone down the street before the garbage truck even got there, and we'd be at school by now.

I wanted to be at school BEFORE Evie got there. If it were my first day of school, I wouldn't want to be there all alone. Maybe from now on Evie could start carpooling with us too. She didn't live exactly on the way to school, but just a little bit out of the way is okay to drive. We have room in the car now since Willa moved away.

I tried pushing myself up in my seat, which wasn't so easy since I was wearing a seat belt. But I wanted to see the garbage truck. Why was it taking so long to load the garbage bags in? This had to be the dirtiest street in all of Somers! I clicked my heels together three times and wished for the garbage truck people to hurry up.

By the time we got to school, Mrs. Finkel had already closed the classroom door. I hate walking into class after everyone else is already there. Actually I've never done it before, but whenever it happens to other kids, everyone turns to look at them.

I pushed open the door and everyone looked at me. Mrs. Finkel looked at her watch. "Did you forget to set your alarm clock?" she asked. Mrs. Finkel is the mean third-grade teacher. The nice teacher, Mrs. Bower, would probably never say something like that.

My face heated up, so I knew I was

blushing. "Our car got stuck behind a garbage truck," I told her.

"Take your seat," Mrs. Finkel said. "We have a new student today and you missed the introduction. Evie, this is Stella Batts. Stella, this is Evie. She just moved here from Great

Britain."

Evie was in Willa's old seat. I hated that Mrs. Finkel was mean to me in front of her, but I gave a little wave.

"We already met this weekend," Evie said. The way she said "weekend" was like this: wee-KEND.

"I was just about to ask for a volunteer to be Evie's buddy," Mrs. Finkel said. "To show her around school and make sure she settles in all right. So Stella, since you already know Evie, will you be her buddy?"

I nodded. Lucy raised her hand and started talking before Mrs. Finkel even called on her. "Actually, I already told Evie I'd show her around."

I thought Mrs. Finkel would get mad at Lucy, because technically talking before you're called on is Disruptive Behavior, but she just said, "That's fine."

No, no, no!!! Wait, wait, wait!!! I wanted to be Evie's buddy! She was supposed to be my new best friend, after all.

I didn't say any of that out loud. I knew there wasn't anything I could do. Mrs. Finkel started teaching. Sometimes what Penny says is really true. It's not fair.

At snack time, I went over to Evie's desk, just like I used to do when Willa was the one sitting there, right in between Lucy and Clark. Other kids had come over too, like Talisa and Arielle and also Joshua, the meanest boy in our whole entire class.

"Where are you from exactly?" Clark asked.

"Duh," Joshua said. "It's so obvious." I don't know why he always comes over to talk to us if he's just going to be mean.

"No, it's not," Clark said. "Mrs. Finkel said Evie was from Great Britain."

"That means London," Joshua said.

"No," Clark said. "Great Britain means England, Scotland, and Wales."

"Really?" I asked. Clark always seems to know stuff like that.

"Yup."

"My dad usually says we're from the UK, short for the United Kingdom, which is Great Britain *and* Northern Ireland," Evie said. "My mom says England. We lived in the city of London."

"See, I told you," Joshua said.

"I love your accent," Talisa told Evie.

"I love yours," Evie said.

"I don't have an accent," Talisa said.

"Yeah you do," Evie said. "An American accent—the same as my mum."

"Her mom is from Somers," I

added, just to be helpful. See, I knew things about Evie that the other kids didn't—that's why I should've been her buddy.

"Can you say something British?" Talisa asked.

"Uh, duh again," Joshua said. "British isn't a language."

"Just so you know, Joshua is the class meanie, so we never listen to him," I told Evie.

Willa would've said that was a mean thing for me to say, but I knew I should tell Evie even if I wasn't her buddy, because I was her new best friend.

There was a knock on the door and we all turned to see who it was—Mrs. Blank from the learning lab. That's where you go if you need extra help. Clark goes there for reading. Mrs. Blank walked over to talk to Mrs. Finkel.

"Knock knock," Talisa said.

"Who's there?" Evie asked.

"Orange."

"Orange who?"

"Orange you glad you don't have to sit next to Joshua?"

"That's very clever," Evie said.

"Thanks," Talisa said. "You want to sit with me at lunch?"

"Sure."

"And me too," I said.

"No, she can't," Lucy cut in before Evie could say anything.

"Why not?" I asked. "She has two sides."

"Yeah, but she has to sit next to me on her other side since I'm her buddy."

"That doesn't mean you have to sit next

to her," I said.

"That's exactly what it means," Lucy said.

"No," I insisted. "You just have to show her around, and when we're eating there won't be anything to show her."

"Pardon me, Stella," Evie said. "But I think I should probably sit next to Lucy."

Mrs. Finkel clapped her hands, which meant it was the part of snack time when we had to sit at our desks.

I raised my hand and Mrs. Finkel called on me. "Can I go to the bathroom?" I asked. I didn't really have to go. I just wanted to be alone. Mrs. Finkel nodded at me. As I walked out the door, she called Evie up to her desk so she could introduce her to Mrs. Blank.

The girls' bathroom is at the end of the hall. I pulled the door open and went into one of the stalls, closed the lid and sat down.

Minutes passed, and then I heard the door open and someone's footsteps. I stood up and flushed the toilet, because that's what you're supposed to do when you're in the bathroom. But I didn't want to leave the stall, so I just sat back down again.

"Hello? Stella?"

It was Arielle's voice. I could tell because it was super soft. But part of wanting to be alone means you don't want to talk to anyone, so I didn't answer. Snack time had to be over by now. What was she doing in the bathroom anyway?

She was quiet for a couple of minutes and I thought maybe she would leave. But then she said, "I know you're in there. I can see your shoes."

I should have folded my legs up right when the door opened. Then she wouldn't be able to see them.

"Are you sick?" she continued. "Maybe you should see the nurse. I can go get her."

If the nurse came, she'd probably call one of my parents to pick me up. That seemed like a pretty good idea.

"Thanks," I said, finally answering her. "But you don't have to get her. I can walk."

I opened the door. Arielle was standing in front of the sink, and she moved over to give me room. I washed my hands, even though I hadn't really gone to the bathroom, because Arielle probably thought I really did and I didn't want to seem gross. Then we walked out into the hall. If you go right, you'll head back toward our classroom. You have to go left to get to the nurse's office.

"I can go with you, if you want," Arielle said.

I shook my head. "No, I'm okay."

The nurse's name is Mrs. Tucker. When I got to her office, I told her I had a stomachache. "Do you think you have to throw up?" she asked.

My stomach felt jumpy, like Pop Rocks were exploding inside of me, but I didn't think I had to throw up until she said it. "Maybe a little bit," I said.

Mrs. Tucker told me to lie down and rest while she called someone to pick me up.

I rolled over and wrapped my arms around my stomach.

A little while later, I felt someone's cool hand on my forehead, and then I heard Mom's voice saying, "You're not feeling well, baby?"

I shook my head under her hand. "I thought Dad would come to get me. You're not supposed to drive."

"Dad's in a meeting," she said. "But don't

worry. I can drive if one of my girls needs me. Come on, let's go home."

I followed her out to the car. Mom squeezed into the front seat. The steering wheel pressed against her stomach. What if the baby could feel it? What if it was hurting the baby? I felt so awful about everything and I started to cry a little bit.

"Oh, Stel, we'll be home soon," Mom said. She thought I was sad about being sick and that made my stomach hurt for real.

CHAPTER 7

Coming Clean

There's a blanket Penny and I like to use whenever we're sick. It looks just like an ordinary blanket, but we call it Magic Blankey. Before I write any more there are two things I want to say about that:

1. I know that's a really babyish name, but that's what we've always called it, starting when I was very little.

2. Obviously it's not really magic. But

sometimes it's nice to pretend, when you're sick.

Whenever Penny or I get sick, Mom takes Magic Blankey out of the hall closet. She spreads it out on the couch in the den, so it's kind of like a bed, and we're allowed to watch whatever we want on TV. The funny thing is, we NEVER use Magic Blankey when we're healthy.

There was a *Superstar Sam* marathon on TV. But I had already seen all the episodes, and I felt weird about lying there watching TV because I knew I wasn't really sick. Now that we were home, my stomach wasn't even jumpy anymore.

What if there was actually something magic about Magic Blankey, and it turned you into the opposite of whatever you were?

Like, if you were sick, you got healthy, and if you were healthy, you got sick.

"I think I'm going to rest in my room," I told Mom. I kicked the blanket off and stood up.

"Do you need anything?" she asked.

She was sitting on the side chair with her feet up on the ottoman. Mom says when you're pregnant, your ankles swell up and

start to hurt. It doesn't really make any sense, since it's not like the baby is in your ankles. But anyway, she looked comfy. Her hands were on her big, blown-up belly, like she was cradling a giant jawbreaker candy. I didn't want to make her move, especially if the baby got hurt from her driving me home.

"No, I'm fine," I told her.

"I'll come check on you later," Mom said.

When I got to my room, I thought maybe I would work on my book. Or maybe I would write a different kind of book—not an autobiography but a short story.

Once upon a time there was a girl whose best friend moved away. She never got another best friend, and so she lived unhappily ever after.

What a sad story. I tried picturing Batts Confections in my head, because sometimes that makes me feel better, except I didn't even know what it looked like, because the candy garden was gone. I ended up taking a nap even though I hadn't even known I was tired. I didn't get up until I heard Mom's voice saying, "I think she may be asleep, but let me check."

When I opened my eyes, Mom was walking toward me. The Magic Blankey was tucked under her arm and the phone was pressed against her ear.

"Oh no, Dave, I think I just woke her," Mom said. She came over and put the blanket down on the bed. I moved my foot so it wasn't touching it.

Mom leaned down to feel my forehead. "She doesn't feel hot, but the nurse said it was her stomach. Let me ask . . . Stel, it's Daddy on

the phone. Do you want to talk to him?"

I shook my head no.

"I don't think she's feeling up to it," Mom said into the phone. She paused. I knew Dad was talking back to her because I could hear muffled sounds coming from the receiver, but it was too fuzzy to make out the exact words.

"I don't think you should bring any treats home if she's sick." She paused again and then said, "Okay. Bye, honey."

She pressed the button to hang up the phone and turned back to me. "Dad's going to keep Penny out for a bit, so it should be peaceful here for a little while longer."

"Where are they?"

"They're dropping Zoey off and then heading to the store. It's closed for the afternoon while the candy circus is installed, and Dad wants to oversee things there."

"I want to go too," I said.

"I know," Mom said. "It's tough to be sick, isn't it?"

I rolled over and smushed my face into my pillow. "But I'm not sick," I said.

"What?" Mom asked. "I can't hear you."

I turned my head so my mouth wasn't

covered up. "I'm not sick," I said. Then I smushed my face back into my pillow.

"Stella," Mom said. Her voice was slightly louder than her regular voice. "Tell me what's going on."

"You're going to be mad," I said into my pillow.

"Look at me," Mom said. "I can't hear you when your face is buried."

I turned my head to Mom again. The jumpiness was back in my stomach. "You're going to be mad," I said again.

"I'm not leaving until you come clean," she said.

So I did.

I started at the beginning—how I called Willa and she didn't want to talk to me. How Dad took us to Man's Best Friend, and I played with the Maltese who I was so sure was meant to be mine. But she wasn't mine–she got sold to someone else. Then Dad brought me over to Evie's house. She didn't like me at first, but then it seemed like maybe *she* would be my new best friend. Except when we got to school she didn't even want to sit with me.

"Oh honey," Mom said. "First of all, I'm sure you misunderstood what Willa was saying."

"I didn't misunderstand," I insisted. "She said she didn't want to talk to me."

"Well then I don't know," Mom said. "But I do know it takes time to make a new best friend. It's not the kind of thing that happens overnight."

"I wish it would," I said. "That's why I said I was sick and you had to come pick me up, even though you're not supposed to drive."

I waited for her to yell at me. But instead

she picked up the phone and punched in some numbers. Was she calling the school to say I'd lied to the nurse?

Someone answered. I could hear a voice, but it was too muffled to hear who it was. "Hey Dave," Mom said. "Can you swing by the house? I think Stella can go with you after all."

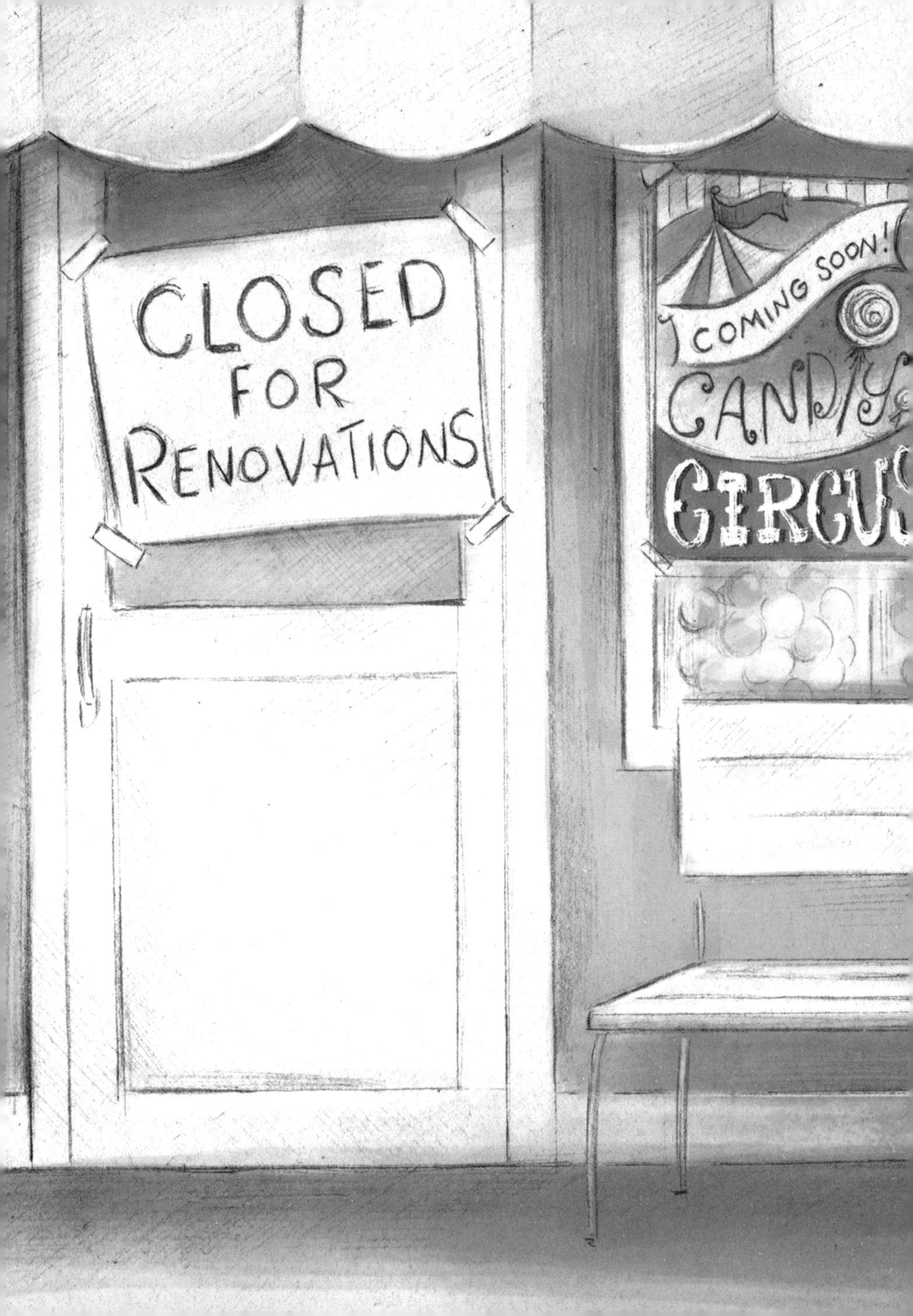
CLOSED FOR RENOVATIONS
COMING SOON!
CANDY
CIRCUS

CHAPTER 8

The Candy Circus

The sign on the door to Batts Confections said "Closed for Renovations." But we just walked right in. Stuart spotted us and called out, "Hey Dave. Hiya, girls."

I know when someone says "hi" to you (or "hiya," like Stuart did), you're supposed to say "hi" back, but Penny and I were too distracted. The candy garden was gone! Of course we knew it was going to be, but when you're used to something looking a certain

way, it's totally weird when it looks completely different.

There was the top of a circus tent hanging from the ceiling. It was striped red and white, like a candy cane. But it didn't go all the way down to the floor like a regular tent. It was just hanging, so you could see what was underneath.

In place of the candy flowers, there was a big red circle on the ground. Then two medium-sized circles, one blue and one yellow, on either side of the red circle. Instead of the chocolate waterfall, there was a red-and-white-striped cart. But wait! We always dipped Oreos in the chocolate fountain! What if I never had an Oreo dipped in chocolate ever again?

Against the wall were a bunch of unpacked boxes, kind of like at Evie's house, except these boxes were marked "lions" and "zebras."

And standing in front of it all was a clown. A mannequin clown, not a real-live clown. He was as tall as Dad and he had rainbow hair and big red circles on his cheeks. His mouth was turned up in a smile, but it was a fake-looking smile, so he didn't actually look happy to see you. And his hands were WAY too big for his body. It was like they were really meant for a giant.

"Whoa," I said.

"Ahhhhhhhhh!!!!" Penny said. "I hate that clown! Get it out of here!"

"See what I mean, Dave?" Stuart asked.

"Daddy, Daddy, we can't stay here," Penny wailed. She attached herself to Dad's leg, and when he took a step closer toward the clown, she yanked on his leg in the other direction so he almost fell over.

"Honey, don't do that," Dad said. "He can't hurt you. He isn't real."

"What if he turns real?" Penny asked.

"That's not possible," Dad said.

"Sure it's possible," Penny insisted. "He could be an evil clown that makes you think he's not real, but then he turns real and . . . and . . ."

"And what?" Dad asked.

"And casts a spell on me so I disappear!"

"He's not a magician," I told her.

"How do you know?" Penny asked. "He could be a clown with two jobs. Mr. Madden the Magician came to the store before, so maybe he heard about it."

"Oh, Penny," Dad said.

"We need to leave RIGHT NOW," she said.

"I have to check the boxes before we go, and figure out how we want the circus set up. You and Stella can help," Dad offered.

"Really?" I asked. I'd helped out at the store before, but never setting up the display that's the FIRST THING you see when you walk in the door.

"I don't want to help," Penny sniffed. "I don't care how it's set up."

"How about this," Dad said. "You and Stella can go upstairs for a little bit while Stuart and I go through the boxes down here."

"We'll keep an eye on the clown and make sure he stays with us," Stuart promised.

"Okay," Penny said. She untangled herself from Dad's leg. Then she came over and grabbed onto my arm with both of her hands. "Let's go upstairs right now," she said.

I still wanted to help out, but I knew I had to take care of Penny. Dad called "thanks" and Penny and I went up to the party room on the second floor. It's decorated like the dining room in a castle. I sat down on the chair at the head of the table. Dad says the chairs are ornate, which means they're very decorative. They're dark and have swirly designs on them.

Penny wandered over to the jelly bean collage that hangs on the wall. It's made to look like a portrait of a king and queen, and she likes to count the jelly beans. But suddenly she ran back to me. "I just thought of something," she said. "What if the clown sneaks away from Dad and Stuart?"

"Stuart said he'd watch the clown," I reminded her.

"Yeah, but what if he's looking in a box and Dad's looking at some other stuff, and the clown sneaks up here and tries to cast a spell on me?"

"I'd jump in front of you so you'd be safe," I said.

"Wow, you're so brave," Penny said.

A few minutes later Dad called out, "Girls! Come on down!"

The boxes were all opened up. Some animals were set up on the circles, but not in any real order. It didn't look like a circus yet. Also there were ropes and Bubble Wrap on the floor.

"Where'd the clown go?" Penny asked, her voice shaking.

"Don't worry," Dad said. "I stuck him in the office downstairs. I don't think we need him anyway."

"I'm never going into your office ever again," Penny told him.

"Maybe one day you'll change your mind," Dad said. "Anyway, Stuart said he could set up the rest of the circus on his own, so we can go."

"Goody!" Penny said. "I don't even like

being in the same building as the clown."

"Take care, Batts family," Stuart said. "I'm in for a long night."

"Can I stay to help you set up?" I asked.

"I'd certainly welcome an assistant," Stuart said. "I can drive you home when we're done. Is that all right, Dave?"

"It's a school night," Dad said. "But Stella can help you for a little bit, as long as she's feeling okay."

"I am!" I said.

"All right. I'll swing back here and pick you up in an hour."

"We'll probably be finished by then, because two people working goes faster than just one," I said.

"That's surely true," Stuart said.

"Okay, kids," Dad said. He calls Stuart a kid, even though I think Stuart is already grown up. He has a job after all. And he calls Dad "Dave," instead of "Mr. Batts," the way other kids do. "I'll see you later. Ready to go, Pen?"

Penny shook her head.

"What's the matter?" Dad asked.

"If Stella stays to help, then I want to."

"Are you sure?" Dad asked.

Penny looked scared, but she reached out to hold my hand and said, "Yes. I want to be brave, like Stella is."

Sometimes I don't mind so much when Penny copies me.

Dad went downstairs to check on a few things in his office, and the three of us got busy unpacking the boxes. There were zebras made of dark chocolate and white chocolate. Penny held up a lion made of hardened sugar. "How did they get this into the right shape?"

she asked.

"I think they must wet the sugar and put it into a lion-shaped mold to let it harden," Stuart said.

"What's this?" I asked, pulling out another chocolate thing. It looked like a bird, sort of. But I'd never been to a circus with birds before.

"Oh, those are the bats. You know, like Batts Confections."

"I don't think bats belong in a circus," I said.

"I suppose you're right," Stuart said. "I just thought it would be fun—chocolate bats at Batts Confections. Maybe we'll save them and have a haunted house one day."

Penny's eyes opened wide.

"Or not," Stuart said. "We can just eat them."

"Can I have one now?" I asked.

"How about we ask your dad when he comes back up," Stuart said. "I don't want you to ruin your appetite for dinner."

It was fun to decide where stuff went. We set all the lions on the blue circle. Two of them sat on little stools, and another was jumping through a mini hula hoop. The lion tamer was standing by with a whip. On the yellow circle,

the bearded lady herded the zebras. Stuart put the red-and-white cart in the middle of the big red circle. He said it was a popcorn machine, and there were lots of different toppings you could put on the popcorn—like

caramel, butterscotch, or crumbled Oreos. It all looked delicious, even if it wasn't a chocolate fountain.

After a little while Dad came upstairs and said it was time to go.

"Can we play with the Bubble Wrap and jump rope first?" Penny asked.

"Actually, that rope is the trapeze," Stuart said. "But it got all tangled up in transit, so I need to untangle it before we hang it up."

"One time my purple necklace got all tangled, and Willa was the only one who could fix it," Penny said.

"She would really like this," I said. "She likes making things look clean and neat. She's the only kid I've ever known who actually LIKES to clean things up!"

"We should've invited her," Stuart said.

"She moved away," Penny said.

"Yeah, and I don't think she likes me anymore," I said.

"Nonsense," Dad said.

"Of course it's nonsense," Stuart said. "Stella Batts is one of the most likeable girls there is!"

"And brave," Penny added. "She said she'd eat a haunted bat!"

"It's just a chocolate bat," I said.

"Stella and me want some, okay Dad?" Penny asked.

"Stella and I," Dad corrected. "And yes, you can take one home for after dinner."

"That gives me an idea," Stuart said. "We have all these unused chocolate bats. What if we made up a care package for your friend Willa? We could send bats for everyone in her family."

"That's five people," Penny interrupted.

"Okay, five bats," Stuart said. "Maybe something is bothering Willa that you just don't know about, and it'll make her feel better to get something sweet. Bats from Miss Batts herself!"

"I like that idea," Dad said. "What do you think, Stel?"

"I think that's okay," I said, though I really wasn't sure how I felt.

CHAPTER 9

Biscuits & Other Things

The next day was Tuesday. Since I wasn't really sick, I had to go to school. Zoey's mom drove us. We got there on time. I sat down at my desk, which is in between the wall and a boy named Spencer. I didn't talk to Evie until it was snack time.

Mom always packs the same snack for me—apple slices and a little piece of candy. Usually it's something from the Penny Candy Wall, but today it was a sliver of Stella's Fudge, which was named after me.

I ate the apples first and then I opened my lunch box to put the apple slices away and get the fudge. The  reason it was just a sliver and not a bigger piece is that Mom packed me dessert too, for when we had lunch. It was two cookies. She'd made them the night before, when Penny and I were at Batts Confections.

"Pardon," a voice said. I knew it was Evie before I even looked up, because she was the only third grader I'd ever heard use that word.

"Yeah?"

"Are you contagious?" she asked.

"What?" I asked.

"Can we catch whatever you have? Is that why you're staying at your desk instead of coming to talk to us?"

"No, I'm all better," I said.

"That's good," she said.

I shut the lid of my lunch box. "Wait," Evie said. "Can I have a biscuit?"

"I don't have any biscuits," I said.

"You don't have to lie about it," she said.

"I'm not lying," I said.

There was a knock on the door. I turned to see Mrs. Blank coming into the room again. "Evie," Mrs. Finkel called. "Do you mind coming over so we can talk about the schedule?"

"Oh, bother," Evie said. Which I guess is the London way of saying, Yes, I do mind. But she had to go, because you can't say that to a teacher.

I popped the fudge into my mouth and sucked on it instead of chewing, so it would last longer. I wondered what subject Evie had to go to learning lab for. It made me feel just the eensy weensiest bit bad for her. If I were the new kid, I wouldn't want everyone thinking I wasn't smart enough and I had to go to the learning lab.

When Mrs. Blank left, Mrs. Finkel clapped her hands. Kids raced around to get back to their desks, but I was already at mine. I clasped my hands together and lifted my arms up over my head. Then I turned my palms upside-down so my knuckles would crack.

"Is anyone done eating?" Mrs. Finkel asked.

I raised my hand. Down

the row, I saw Evie raising her hand, too.

"Mrs. Blank left her planner behind, so I need a volunteer to take it back to her room."

Behind me I heard Joshua saying, "Oooh, oooh, oooh," which is the sound he makes when he's waving his hand around.

"Yes, Joshua?" Mrs. Finkel asked.

Joshua said something that sounded like, "Whoomp whoomp whoomp."

"It looks like you just stuffed the rest of your snack into your mouth," Mrs. Finkel said. "It's hard to understand you."

"I said I'll take it," Joshua said.

"I saw Stella's hand first."

Joshua slammed his hand down on his desk, which is what he does when he's upset about something. "That's enough, Joshua," Mrs. Finkel said. "Stella, will you take the planner for me?"

"Sure," I said. It's cool to run errands for your teacher.

"And Evie, was that a hand up saying you were done?"

Evie nodded.

"All right, Stella, take Evie with you, so she can see Mrs. Blank's office."

I guess that sort of made me Evie's buddy. The thing is, I didn't want that job anymore. But I said okay, because you can't say no to a teacher, either.

Mrs. Finkel handed me the planner and Evie and I walked out to the hall. "I already finished my snack because I forgot to bring one," she told me. "We didn't have snack time at my old school. That's why I asked for a biscuit."

"I really didn't have any," I said.

"But I saw them," she insisted. "If you sit next to me at lunch today, I'll prove it to you."

"Don't you have other people to sit with?" I asked.

"You just want me to sit with other people because you have the biscuits and you don't want me to see."

"That's not true," I said. "You picked other people to sit with yesterday, so I thought you wouldn't want to sit with me."

"That's because I didn't know those kids and I already knew you. When we first moved here, I didn't want to make new friends because I missed my old ones so much. But then I met you, and you were really nice, so

I wanted to meet more people. Now I know everyone, and I'd like to sit with you. If that's okay."

"Yeah, that's okay," I said. I smiled, just the eensy weensiest little bit. Now she knew everyone–and she was picking me.

We got to the learning lab. I gave Mrs. Blank her planner back. "Thanks," she said. "Au revoir, Evie. À lundi."

"Au revoir," Evie said.

I happen to know that "au revoir" is French for "goodbye," because once on *Superstar Sam*, Sam had a gymnastics meet in France. But I didn't know the other words.

"What did Mrs. Blank say to you?" I asked, once Evie and I were back in the hallway.

"That she'd see me on Monday. I'm starting French lessons in the learning lab."

"But we don't have language classes until

fourth grade," I said. Fourth grade is still a year away. Then we get to pick French or Spanish.

"I know," Evie said. "But we already started French at my old school in London. My parents don't want me to skip a year."

"Oh that's cool," I said. "I wish I could learn French now."

"I'll teach you some if you want."

"How do you say, 'See you at lunch'?"

"Je te verrai à midi," Evie said.

I tried to repeat it, but I don't think it sounded quite right.

We got back to our classroom. Mrs. Finkel had already started our social studies lesson, so Evie and I went straight to our desks.

An hour and a half later, it was lunchtime. Evie sat in the seat next to me and I opened up my lunch box. "You see," I said. "All I have is a turkey-and-cheese sandwich, a juice box, and—"

"And biscuits!" she said.

"Those aren't biscuits," I said. "Those are chocolate-chip cookies."

"That's not what we call them in London," Evie said.

All of a sudden I thought of something. "Last week, when I saw you outside Man's Best Friend and you were going to eat at Brody's Grill, you said you wanted a 'plate of chips,' but you didn't really mean chips, did you?"

"They're called something else in America," Evie said. "I can't remember the name. But they're made of potatoes and they're long and skinny. You get them with burgers."

"Oh, you mean French fries!" I said.

"That's it," Evie said.

"I have an idea," I said. "I'll teach you the American words for things, and you can teach me French."

"Yeah," Evie said. "And I can teach you British words too."

"But then you're teaching me two and I'm only teaching you one," I said.

"I don't mind," Evie said.

She held out her hand. We shook to make it official.

CHAPTER 10

Best Friends

Dad was there when Evie and I walked out of school at the end of the day, since it was his turn to do carpool. Penny and Zoey were with him. They're in kindergarten, and they get out a few minutes earlier.

Evie's mom was standing with Dad too, and you'll never guess who she was holding in her arms. Malty!

"Surprise!" Mrs. King said.

"It's Malty!" Penny shrieked.

"Bella!" Evie said, reaching for her.

"You see," Dad told me. "I told you she'd end up in a good home."

"How did you know if they just got her today?"

"Actually," Mrs. King said, "I got her on Saturday morning, right when I ran into your dad at the shopping center. But I didn't want to bring her home until we'd unpacked. The house was too messy to be safe for a puppy. It's still a bit messier than I'd like."

"You should've seen the mess the puppy made at our house!" Penny said.

"Not really," I said quickly. "Malty isn't a bad dog. We were just pretending."

"Why do you keep calling her Malty?" Evie asked.

"That's what Stella named her," Penny said.

"We played with her at Man's Best Friend last week," I explained. "It's because she's a Maltese. And also because I like the malted candies—you know, like Maltesers and malt balls."

"That can be her middle name," Evie said. "Bella Malty. What do you think?"

"I think it's really good," I said.

"Mom, can Stella come over today?" Evie asked.

"That's up to Stella," Mrs. King said. "And Stella's dad."

"Please, Dad?" I asked.

"Sure," Dad said. "But I told Willa's mom that you'd call Willa back when I picked you up, so why don't you come for a ride with me, and I'll bring you to Evie's after I drop Penny and Zoey."

Then we got into the car and Dad handed

me his cell phone. My stomach felt jumpy all over again. I dialed Willa's number. The phone started ringing and Mrs. Getter answered. "This is Stella Batts," I said.

"Hold on a sec, Stel," Mrs. Getter said. "Let me get Willa."

THUMP THUMP THUMP went my heart. What if she said "I don't want to talk to her" again?

But then I heard a voice say "Hi Stella"— and it was Willa's voice!

"Hi," I said. My voice came out way softer than it usually sounds. It was more like Arielle's voice. So then I said, "It's Stella." That way Willa would know for sure.

"I've been waiting for you to call," she said.

"I called the other day, but you said you didn't want to talk to me," I told her.

"How did you know I said that?"

"I heard you through the phone," I told her.

"Are you mad at me?" she asked.

"I wasn't mad," I said. "Just sad. I thought you didn't want to be my best friend. Then Evie didn't want to be my friend, but that's okay now."

"Who's Evie?"

"She's the new girl in school."

"Oh, that's weird," Willa said.

"What's weird?"

"That there's a girl in school I don't even know."

"But you moved away," I reminded her.

"So Evie's your best friend now?"

"No," I said. "It takes time to make a best

friend. YOU'RE still my best friend. It's okay to have a best friend that lives far away. We just have to talk on the phone more."

"So maybe Evie can be your second best friend," Willa said.

"Yeah," I said. "Maybe she can be that."

"I'm sorry I didn't talk to you the other day. Sometimes I just get upset when I think too much about Somers. I miss it so much, so then I pretend I never lived there."

"Evie misses her old home so much that at first she didn't even want to be my friend," I told Willa.

"You can be friends with her," Willa said. "But I'm glad you're still my best friend."

We talked for a few more minutes. She told me

some things about Pennsylvania and I filled her in on what was going on in Somers. Then Dad pulled up in front of Hilltop Acres and it was time to go. "By the way, you're going to get a surprise from me in the mail."

"Really? What is it?"

"I can't tell you, or else it won't be a surprise."

"Okay, well I'll call you as soon as I get it."

"Call me even before then."

"I'll call you before then," Willa agreed.

We said goodbye and hung up. Evie was standing on the sidewalk with Malty—I mean Bella Malty—in her arms, waiting for me. I handed Dad back his cell phone and rushed out to meet them.

Sneak preview of

Stella Batts

A Case of the Meanies

Book

Story Ingredients

"Stella, can you come here a minute?" Mrs. Finkel asked.

I went up to Mrs. Finkel's desk. This girl Maddie's story was at the top of the pile of story lists. Mrs. Finkel had written ✔ on the top. Checks are what we get on most of our assignments. It means "This is good work."

Mrs. Finkel thumbed through the pile and pulled out my paper. She tapped it with her pencil. It didn't have a check mark on it.

"Are you sure you understood the assignment?" she asked.

"Yes," I said.

"It's all right if you didn't," Mrs. Finkel said. "I know this is third grade and you're just learning about how to write a story."

"Actually I've written lots of books," I told her.

Okay, only three. But that's a lot for an eight year old! That may be even more than Mrs. Finkel has written!

"You didn't give much of a plot description," Mrs. Finkel said.

"That's because you don't get to know the end of a story until you read it." *Duh*, I wanted to tell her, like Joshua would. But I'd never say that to a teacher. I'd never say that to anyone.

Okay, maybe I'd say it to Penny. But she's my little sister, and things you say to your little sister are different than things you'd say to anyone else.

"That's part of story writing," Mrs. Finkel said. "The author gets to know what happens at the end before the readers do. It's okay to put those details here, though, for this assignment."

"But not everything has happened yet."

"I see," Mrs. Finkel said. *I see* is another way grown-ups say *I understand*. But the way Mrs. Finkel was looking at me, kind of frowning so she got a little wrinkle between her eyes, I could tell she didn't really understand at all.

She picked up the whole pile of kids' papers and shuffled them together so the edges matched up. "Why don't you do the honor of handing these back to your classmates?"

I shrugged my shoulders. "Okay," I said.

"Think about the plot a bit at home tonight. Maybe you'll be inspired. Do you know what that word means?"

Of course I did! It's when something gives you the feeling to want to do something. Things inspire me to write my books all the time.

"Yes, I know what the word means," I told Mrs. Finkel.

"We can discuss it again tomorrow, if you want," she said.

I knew I would NOT want to do that. Mrs. Finkel handed me the pile and I went around the room, giving each paper back to the right person. Every single kid had a check mark on top of his or her page. Some kids even had a check plus, which is what Mrs. Finkel writes when she thinks our work is better than just fine.

Joshua's list was the last in the pile. Even he had a check mark. I handed it over to him.

"I saw Penny in the principal's office," he said. "That's what I wanted to tell you."

Courtney Sheinmel

Courtney Sheinmel is the author of several books for middle-grade readers, including *Sincerely* and *All The Things You Are*. Like Stella Batts, she was born in California and has a younger sister. However, her parents never owned a candy store. Now Courtney lives in New York City, where she has tasted all the cupcakes in her neighborhood. She also makes a delicious cookie brownie graham-cracker pie. Visit her at www.courtneysheinmel.com, where you can find the recipe along with information about all the Stella Batts books.

Jennifer A. Bell

Jennifer A. Bell is a children's book illustrator whose work can also be found in magazines, on greeting cards, and on the occasional Christmas ornament. She studied Fine Arts at the Columbus College of Art and Design and currently lives in Minneapolis, Minnesota.

In this early chapter book series, the ups and downs of Stella's life are charmingly chronicled. She's in third grade, she wants to be a writer, and her parents own a candy shop. Life should be sweet, right?

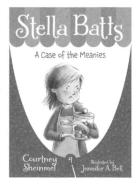